"REFRESHI

❝ *Lincoln Park* provides a refreshing and innovative way to nurture the spirituality of young adolescents. The characters and situations they encounter explore common questions and concerns that weave life and faith into an adventure of *being* and *believing* for your adolescents. **❞**

Mary Lee Becker, *Young Adolescent Ministry Consultant*

❝ I loved the way I had to search for hidden messages throughout this book. It gave me time to think about the choices they were making. I felt like I could relate because of the up-to-date situations. **❞**

Alysa, age 14

ABOUT THE AUTHORS

John Shea

John (Jack) Shea is a theologian and storyteller who lectures nationally and internationally on storytelling in world religions, faith-based health care, contemporary spirituality, and the spirit at work movement.

Jack was previously a professor of systematic theology and the Director of the Doctor of Ministry Program at the University of St. Mary of the Lake, a research professor at the Institute of Pastoral Studies at Loyola University of Chicago, and the Advocate Healthcare Senior Scholar in Residence at the Park Ridge Center for the Study of Health, Faith and Ethics. He has also taught at the University of Notre Dame and Boston College.

Jack has published thirteen books of theology and spirituality and two books of poetry.

Mike Carotta

An author and nationally renowned speaker, Dr. Michael Carotta has worked with adolescents and their spiritual growth in educational, pastoral, and clinical settings for more than twenty-five years. A long time educator, Mike has also served as Diocesan Director of Adolescent Catechesis, Executive Director of the NCEA Department of Religious Education, and Director of Religious Education at Girls and Boys Town in Omaha, Nebraska.

Author of more than forty articles and six books, Michael's work has appeared in a variety of publications. He regularly teaches graduate courses on adolescent spirituality and catechesis at Boston College, Loyola University of New Orleans, St. John's School of Theology in Minnesota, and Fordham University in New York.

LINCOLN PARK
All S.O.U.L.s

Printed in the United States of America

ISBN 0-15-901906-0

2 3 4 5   076   11 10 09

CHAPTER 1

OTHER ARTISTS

"This is the last one," gasped the guy in the pirate mask.

He was out of breath. It was late Halloween Eve, just before midnight, and he and his companions had been running through Lincoln Park from tunnel to tunnel—leaving their messages on the walls.

"I hate to see the fun stop." The words came out of the gnarled lips of a Frankenstein mask.

The other two, Mickey Mouse and Superwoman, laughed, but said nothing.

Then all four turned their flashlights on the walls. For a moment they were silent, the beams crisscrossing, lighting up the explosion of images.

"What is this?" said the Pirate.

Superwoman pulled a scrap of paper from her jeans pocket. The beam from her flashlight moved down the page.

"We've done Great Americans, World of Animals, Children Count, Workers of the World, and Family Life. This must be Spiritual Heritage."

The flashlights went back to their work, exploring the walls.

"Here's a cross," said Mickey Mouse. "But it's got flowers on it. It's not burning."

"There's the Jew star of David," grumbled Frankenstein.

"Here's that pregnant Mexican Mary." Superwoman had spotted her.

"There's a black jerk with his arms out," said Mickey Mouse.

They all turned to the Pirate.

"This stuff is exactly what we hate," he told them.

For the sixth time that night, the Halloween tricksters pulled spray paint cans from their pockets. Ten minutes later, when the last of the paint sputtered out, they were breathing heavily. Their effort had taken everything out of them.

Then they stood in the middle of the tunnel and slowly turned, reviewing the damage with their flashlights.

"Alright!" said Frankenstein.

"Better than alright!" said the Pirate.

Frankenstein, Superwoman, and Mickey Mouse basked in the Pirate's praise.

Superwoman knew it was time. She positioned the flashlights, took the camera from her pack, and had the Pirate, Frankenstein, and Mickey line up in front of the words they had scrawled on the walls.

"Now smile," she said.

It was the sixth time that night she had said that. And for the sixth time they laughed again, safely hiding behind their masks.

The night raid was over. They clicked off their flashlights and began walking toward the front of the tunnel that led out of Lincoln Park Zoo. But some instinct made them suddenly run, each step taking them into the largeness of the city where their deeds could not be traced.

ONE WEEK EARLIER

CHAPTER 2

THE SOULS GATHER

"Everybody listen up," senior Dana Cali shouted.

The October SOULs' meeting was being called to order and the seniors were in charge.

Derrick Lamay waited until everyone was quiet. "We're going back to Lincoln Park in a week to help with the Children's Halloween Party."

What will we be doing?" asked Alvin.

"Whatever they need us to do," Dana shrugged. "Probably help with the games. Serve food. Clean up afterwards."

Robbie raised his hand. "What happens if you can't make it?"

The seniors looked to Ms. Allister.

"If a person can't make it, he or she needs to have a really good reason," said Ms. A.

"I'm supposed to go to my aunt's wedding. My uncle and I are both in the wedding party."

"Does that mean you have to wear a tux?" asked Alvin.

"Sounds like a good reason," said Ms. A. "Plus you can always find out what we did and put it on the website."

"How is the website?" asked Ben Alvarez.

"It's good. I took Ms. A's mom's yearbook from last month's meeting and scanned in the pictures of the three kids who started SOUL. I wanted to remind all the other SOULs in America that it all began here at the K."

"Nice," said Ellen Linh.

"But I don't know what else to do with the website, so if anyone has any ideas let me know."

"How's the coin?" asked Derrick with a smile.

"Okay I guess. But it's driving me crazy trying to figure out where it came from."

"Wrong question," said Ms. A.

"I know," said Robbie, "but it's still bothering me."

"There's your website stuff," said Ellen. "Tell the story on the website and see if other SOULs can help you figure out the answer."

"Ms. A?" asked Robbie.

"Sure, as long as you agree to answer the more important question."

The SOULs suddenly became silent as they looked at Robbie. They were waiting to hear what that question was.

"*Why* did I get it?" Robbie sighed.

Robbie was frustrated by both questions. How and why was he now carrying a coin in his pocket that he couldn't spend? And he didn't like the spotlight. People were always asking to see it and, of course, everyone kept asking him how he got it—and why he got it. So he decided to take the heat off himself.

"You know Kate had something strange happen to her, too." Robbie didn't look at Kate when he said it, but everyone else did.

Kate was caught off guard. She didn't want any more attention either. She was just happy Ms. A hadn't already kicked her out.

"Do you want to tell us, Kate? No pressure," said Ms. A.

Kate was silent for a moment. Then she thought about how Ms. A had cut her some slack. Maybe this could be a way for her to bounce back from her past mistakes.

"It's a puzzle, a lot like Robbie's."

Kate explained the whole thing quickly, from skipping out to buy jewelry—which everyone already knew—and losing her backpack in the lake, which everyone also knew. But then she continued with what no one but Robbie knew.

She told the other SOULs about the strange question an elderly lady on the bus had asked her. Kate's eyes widened and her voice took on a "Can you believe it?" tone as she described how her backpack showed up on her front doorstep the next day, still wet and with everything in it. There had been a note on it asking the same question, "Isn't wisdom more precious than silver and gold?"

Kate sat back shaking her head, still amazed by everything that had happened to her.

"Strange."

"Cool."

"Freaky."

"Awesome."

"Was the note signed?" asked Alvin.

Kate laughed, "No! The question is, how did it get there? It was at the bottom of the lagoon, remember?"

"Wrong question," insisted Ms. A for the second time in the meeting. "What's the answer to the question, 'Isn't wisdom more precious than silver and gold?'"

"I know what I'm supposed to say." Kate said dryly. "Everybody knows a set-up question when they hear it. Wisdom is more precious than silver and gold. But I really don't know what wisdom is, so if I said that I'd just be a . . ." Kate hesitated and just shook her head.

"Stay with it. Things will happen and you will see," encouraged Ms. A.

"What things?" asked Alvin.

Ms. A didn't even look at him. "You okay with that, Kate?"

"I guess." Kate shrugged.

Ms. A glanced at her watch.

Dana took the hint. "We have two new SOULs with us today. Would you please introduce yourselves?"

A thin girl stood up in the back.

"I'm Kim Su Vans and I'm a freshman on the JV volleyball team. I couldn't make the last meeting, and stuff, but our season ends next week and I have to join a club, so here I am."

"Where are you from?" asked Ellen.

"Longwood Middle School." Kim Su replied.

"No, I mean what country?"

"Oh, Korea. Sorry."

"I'm from Taiwan, that's why I asked," said Ellen, smiling. "Glad you're with us."

Dana looked at another new SOUL and he stood up.

"I'm Serge Henbatis. I'm also a freshman. I'm on the JV soccer team. Our season ends in one week also, so, I too, need to join a club for the rest of the year."

"I've heard about you," said Ben. "They say you can play."

"Thanks. I've been playing since I was three. In Iraq, where I'm from."

"How long have you been here?" asked Ben.

"Five years. My family came to Chicago when I was nine. For safety."

"Serious?"

"Yes. We had to leave or be killed. Now we are citizens here. Thank you." Serge sat down.

"What's it like being in this country?" asked Alvin.

"For another time, Alvin," said Ms. A.

Derrick wrapped things up. "Okay, that's it. Our thirty minutes are up. Everyone needs to be in front of the school on Halloween at nine in the morning. We work from ten until two. Grab a permission slip before you leave and bring it back to Ms. A, signed. Any questions?" he asked.

One hand shot up.

"Does anyone besides Alvin have any questions?"

Everyone laughed.

But Alvin called out his question over the laughter. "Are we supposed to wear costumes?"

CHAPTER 3

HELP

"One of the SOULs here at the K—a freshman—found a SOUL coin among the loose change from the pockets of his shorts and jacket. He doesn't know how it got there, but he's trying hard to figure it out. So for all you SOULs out there who want to help, here's the full story . . ."

It was early morning, an hour before classes began, and Robbie was perched in front of a computer at the back of the library. He stopped typing to re-read what he had just posted on the SOUL of The K website. It looked good. He was seeking help from other SOULs on how the coin could have gotten into his pocket. But he had decided to disguise the fact that it had happened to him. It would be the story of an anonymous freshman. He already had all the attention he could take.

"Mr. Matthews, you must like it here in the library."

Robbie swiveled the chair around.

"Good morning, Msfits."

"Doing SOUL work again?" she asked, glancing at the computer screen.

"Yes ma'am." Robbie left it at that.

"I heard you had an exciting trip to the zoo."

"Yes ma'am."

"I also heard you received a coin."

"Yes, ma'am."

Msfits sat at the computer next to where Robbie was working. Apparently she was staying.

Robbie knew what she was waiting for. He pulled the coin out of his pocket and handed it to her. "Bet you've seen a bunch of these, huh?"

"Still special every time I see one." She smiled as she studied the coin closely.

Robbie decided to take a chance. "I don't know how I got this coin. I'm typing up the story for the website to see if I can get some help from other SOULs. Ms. A said I could."

"It's always a bit of a puzzle, isn't it? I'm sure there will be no shortage of suggestions about how you got this. But, of course, that's not the right question, is it?"

"Ms. A's already reminded me, *why* did I get it? But I don't know how or why I got this coin, and I don't think I can figure it out. I think it might have been a mistake. Plus, I'm getting all this attention I don't want. And people are saying that now I have to watch others and know when to give the darn thing away."

"That feels better, doesn't it?" Msfits smiled. "Getting it out like that."

Robbie nodded.

"You'll eventually know why. You just need some help. I like it that you went to other SOULs to see if they could figure out how the coin got into your possession. But you need a different kind of help to figure out why you received it."

"What kind?"

"The kind of help that's on the coin."

Msfits handed the coin back to Robbie. "Tell me what you see on the coin."

Robbie read off three words, "Truth, Beauty, Love." He turned the coin over, "See, Judge, Act."

"Anything else?" asked Msfits.

Robbie looked again at both sides. "There's an angel at the top."

Msfits looked into Robbie's eyes and her voice was forceful and instructive. "Angels are often sent to help people. They help by providing higher wisdom. You need higher wisdom to know why you received the coin."

Msfits saw that Robbie was confused.

"I suspect you followed a Truth and came to new level of understanding," she explained.

"I don't even know what happened," Robbie protested. "How can I have followed Truth into a . . .?" His voice trailed off.

"Truth isn't knowing what happened," Msfits said.

"Then what is it?" Robbie asked.

Msfits caught Robbie's eyes and held them in her own steady gaze, "Truth is knowing yourself."

CHAPTER 4

WOMAN TO WOMAN

"Hello?"

Kate was sprawled on the couch watching television when her cell phone rang. She checked the caller ID but didn't recognize the area code.

"So how's your new school?" asked the voice on the other end.

Kate's stomach knotted, her face flushed with anger, and a hard edge entered her voice. She jerked up off the couch and began to pace.

"Hi Dad," she said.

"I haven't heard from you in a few months so I was wondering how you were doing. You decided to go to Kennedy right?"

"Yup. I'm at Kennedy." She didn't want to tell him anything more. She was too hurt. If he hadn't left the family a year ago and moved away over some stupid mid-life crisis thing, then he would know everything about her.

"Is it hard?" he asked.

"Not really."

"Are you liking it?"

"Pretty much." She started to ask him about what was going on in his life, but stopped herself on purpose.

Silence. A long, awkward, silence

Finally her dad spoke up. "How's Eric?"

"Maybe you should ask him yourself," she said sarcastically. Immediately she knew she hurt her father's feelings.

Eric did not have a cell phone. To talk to Eric he would have to call the house at night. That meant Mom would pick up and he would have to talk to her.

"I guess you're right."

"I know I'm right," Kate blurted before her dad could finish. "You haven't spoken to Eric in months."

"I just wanted to tell you that I've been thinking about you and your first year in high school."

"Gotta let you go now, Dad, have to take . . ."

"See ya, Kate." Her dad said before she could finish. He knew an excuse was coming.

Kate heard the click of the receiver and the hum of the dial tone. She dropped the phone on the couch and turned off the television. She put her hands over her face and for the millionth time the same questions ran through her mind. *Why did he have to leave? Was it really that bad between him and Mom? What was his problem? Was it me or Eric that pushed him out? Why did Mom just say mid-life crisis and clam up?*

Just then she heard Mom and Eric come through the front door. Soccer practice was over.

"Hi Sis!" Eric smiled. He always smiled when he saw her after school. Kate looked at her mom. "Dad just called."

"Is he still on the phone?" Eric asked excitedly.

"No, he had to go," Kate fibbed. She knew her dad would still be on the phone to talk to Eric if she hadn't been so short with him.

Eric's shoulders slumped. He trudged off to his room.

"What'd he say?" asked Mrs. D.

"Nothing. Just wanted to know how school was. Told him things were fine."

Mrs. D knew her daughter. There was something different in the way she answered. "Kate?"

Kate turned to walk away.

"Kate!"

She turned back.

"What happened?"

"I told him that he should call Eric. That he hadn't spoken to Eric in months."

"And what did your dad say?"

"I told him I had to go."

"You cut him off, Kate?"

Kate ignored the question.

"Why did he have to leave Mom? Tell me the truth and don't sugarcoat it. Just tell me why he couldn't stay."

"It was a mid-life thing," said Mrs. D calmly. Shortly after the separation, she had made up her mind not to be bitter and complain about him in front of their children.

"Mom! That's not an answer," Kate raised her voice, "What does that mean?"

Mrs. D turned away from the question and walked toward the kitchen. Kate pursued her. In the kitchen Mrs. D sat down wearily. Kate took the chair opposite her.

"There is no good reason," Mrs. D finally said. "Your dad left because he felt that he was going to miss out on the rest of his life by staying here with me. He felt that he was dying by not doing what he really wanted to be doing. He said that he wanted to live the rest of his life his own way, moving to a part of the country where he always wanted to live, taking the kind of job he really wanted to do, and being free of the responsibilities that came with being with me."

"You mean he didn't want to miss out on the rest of his life staying here with US. He wanted to be free of the responsibilities that came with taking care of US!" Kate's voice was strong, convinced of what she was saying.

"No. It wasn't about you and Eric."

"Yes it was. How could it not be? He was stuck with us! Responsible for us!"

"It was *not* like that," her mom insisted.

"Then maybe it should have been! He helped put us here. We didn't bring ourselves into this world. He brought us here and then he walked out on us. That's the point, Mom. Maybe it should've been about US! Maybe he should have thought about US!"

"Mid–life . . . ," but Mrs. D did not get to say more.

Kate pushed away from the table.

"Let me finish Kate!"

Kate sat back down, but she was in no mood for dancing around the subject, nice nice.

"People get scared in mid-life. Some people focus only on themselves. Some say it's like becoming a teenager all over again. It's like a 'What do I want to do with my life?' kind of thing, only this time it comes with a real fear—almost a panic—like 'I better hurry because I don't have much time left!' Kate, I'm not saying it's a good reason. I'm just trying to explain it."

"Mom, it's lame. It's like you're defending him. Aren't you mad at him? I hate him."

The kitchen was quiet. Kate waited.

Inside Mrs. D it felt like the "protective mother" switch just clicked off. She looked into the eyes of the young woman opposite her, considering how much she wanted to say.

"I ran out of 'mad' and 'angry' a couple of months ago. As for hate, be careful. It can consume you."

Mrs. D said it matter-of-factly, not in a motherly tone, just a warning from one woman to another. And she wasn't finished.

"I'm numb now. Not feeling much. Sometimes you think that if you know the reasons, you'll be able to handle it. But what if there are no reasons or the reasons are not the real reasons? What if you sense there is something else but you can't get at it? And you scream and shout and you still don't know. Then you have to live with the results without the reasons. That's where I'm at, Kate. I'm trying not to obsess about figuring it out. Just 'let it go' I tell myself, and get on with life."

Mrs. D's voice sounded like it came from a place of exhaustion, a place where she didn't want to be but a place she knew very well.

"Mom," Kate said, finally feeling she was really talking to her mother. "I can't let it go. I'm too angry."

"Time will help."

"I'm not sure time *will* help." Kate shook her head.

"Then pray you find some way to let it go."

CHAPTER 5

EVERYBODY'S
DIFFERENT

"Everybody here?" asked Jamie Allister.

"Everybody who's anybody." Derrick answered, just like he did when Ms. A asked the same question last month.

"How about the two new freshmen?"

"Kim Su and Serge are here," said Dana. "But Robbie isn't here. He's at a wedding. Remember?"

"Right. Let's head to the bus stop, people!" Ms. A shouted, taking the last of the permission slips.

With that, the SOUL of The K was on its way to the second project of the year. It was a chilly Saturday morning, but the sky was clear and the sun shone so brightly it shimmered off the shiny yellow surface of the bus.

The four freshmen sat together, partially for their own comfort and partially because no one else would sit with them. Kate sat next to Kim Su and Alvin sat next to Serge.

"So how did soccer end up?" Alvin asked Serge.

"Very good. I think the coach was happy."

"Do you miss your homeland?"

"I do not miss it. America is nice. But the customs are strange."

"Like what?"

Serge was suspicious about questions. Sometimes, even innocent questions made him wonder if someone was trying to get information to use against him.

"You ask a lot of questions. Why?" Serge asked.

Not knowing what to say, Alvin just shrugged and turned to look out the window.

Kate was looking out of the window too. The same neighborhood as last time passed before her eyes; she saw the same beautiful women, some in their baseball hats jogging with their purebred dogs, some sipping coffee with their friends at the corner Starbucks, all dressed in their designer clothes and sunglasses.

But this time she also saw people huddled in doorways. Others were pushing grocery carts with all of their worldly possessions in them. The poor and homeless were mixed in with the rich and trendy. The sight of both—side by side—caught Kate's attention.

"There's more homeless people around here than I thought. I didn't notice them last month," Kate said to Kim Su.

"I wasn't here last time. But even if I was, it wouldn't matter." Kim Su replied with a shrug of her shoulders.

"Why doesn't it matter?"

"Poor people are always around, even when you don't see them. They've given up the fight. They don't want to make it work."

"What?"

"Poor people are poor because they don't hustle."

"Tell that to a single mom, trying to feed her kids without a husband," Kate said.

Kim Su shrugged again.

The shrug angered Kate. "A single mom who has to take the bus to work. A single mom who has to work the 3 to 11 shift every night. Tell that to her kids who have to make their own supper, do their homework without a computer or any adult helping them. Tell that to the oldest kid who has to make sure the younger ones take their baths and get their clothes ready for the next day. Tell them that they are poor because they don't hustle."

Kim Su turned completely sideways, faced Kate, and told her the truth as though she had repeated it to herself many times. "My family came here with no money. Couldn't even speak the language. My uncles and aunts, my grandparents, my parents, and my brothers and sisters. All of us. We all worked hard. We helped each other. We're surviving and making it. We don't give up."

"Okay. I get it," Kate admitted. "But your family had a big *we*. Some poor people have no one to help them. The single mom has no *we*. Suppose you and your brothers and sisters just had your mom. Nobody else. No *we*. Think things would have turned out the same?"

Kim Su thought about it for a second. "We still would've hustled and made it. These people don't work hard enough." She was not convinced by Kate.

There was something in the way that Kim Su said "these people" that sent a chill through Kate.

"*These people*? That's prejudiced. You think all *these people* are lazy don't you? You need to cut *these people* some slack."

Kim Su shrugged again.

Determined not to let it go, Kate tapped Serge, who was sitting in the row in front of them, on the shoulder. "Do you think poor people are poor because they don't hustle?"

Serge turned around. "Poor people are poor because of many things. Some cannot get to work because they have no transportation or money for transportation."

"But they would make transportation money from their jobs," Kim Su was back in the conversation.

"Not after they pay for the food and the electricity their family needs. Plus the rent money," Serge replied. "I have seen it many times."

"Are there a lot of poor people in Iraq?" asked Alvin.

"Many people are poor. And many of the poor were the hardest workers in Iraq," said Serge.

"What type of work do most people do?" continued Alvin, eager for more information.

It was another Alvin-kind-of-question, and it lessened the tension. Kate and Kim Su smiled. Serge laughed. Then they all went silent.

Kate turned and looked out the window. The bus was passing Angela's Jewelry Boutique. She wasn't as interested in it as she was the last time. Silver and gold jewelry weren't calling out to her anymore.

Something else was.

CHAPTER 6

RESTORATION

"We should have worn our costumes," Alvin said to Serge, as he looked at the park decorated for Halloween.

Goblins and witches were hanging from lampposts. The Information Center had been turned into a haunted house. Kids in costumes were lining up in front of the booths and games. Even the parents, who stood a few steps back and watched their children, had on a wig or a nose or a hat that made them part of Halloween.

But Ms. A did not notice any of that.

"Something's not right," she said out loud to everyone.

Two police cruisers with their red and blue lights flashing were parked next to the haunted house. Off to one side was Carl Howard, the chief assistant for City Councilwoman Martha Gray. He was talking to the police.

Ms. A recognized him from last month's event and walked toward him. The SOULs followed.

"Good to see you again, Ms. Allister," Carl Howard said sincerely. "Are you and your students flexible this morning?"

"Sure. What do you need?"

"As you might have guessed by the police, we have a crime scene on our hands. Someone spray painted all the tunnels in the park last night as a Halloween Trick or Treat prank. We just discovered it about an hour ago. The park's maintenance crew says the vandals used a water based spray paint. It can be washed away without hurting the oil based paint beneath."

"Okaaay . . ." Ms. A drew out the word not sure what he was getting at.

"Would your group be willing to wash the spray paint off the tunnels today instead of working the games at the Children's Halloween Party?"

For Jamie Allister this was a no-brainer. But she had stressed the need for the SOULs to pay attention after last month's trip. So she turned to the seniors. "Your call," she told them.

Dana, Ben, Derrick, and Ellen all looked at each other for a second. Ellen and Ben nodded slightly; then they all did.

"Let's do it." Ellen said.

"Thank you!" Mr. Howard replied looking relieved. "The city is grateful. We put a lot of time, money, and planning into renovating these tunnels. And the artists have done a great job. Cleaning them up is important to us and the visitors. With your help we can get it all done today."

"How do we do it?" asked Alvin, earning a look from Ben.

Mr. Howard called over the Park Supervisor. They talked privately for a moment, and then the Park Supervisor turned toward the SOULs.

"Glad you guys are here. There are six tunnels. My people can probably clean three. If you can divide up and take the other three, then we can have this all done today."

Jamie Allister instinctively started to divide up the group. But the teacher inside her told her not to. Again, she looked at the seniors. It took them a few seconds to figure out that this too was their call.

"Since we don't have any sophomores this year, seniors, juniors, and freshmen can each take a tunnel," said Dana.

"Which tunnel is the biggest?" Derrick asked the Park Supervisor.

"Workers of the World."

"Then, that's the juniors' tunnel since there are five of them here. The four seniors and the four freshmen will take any two tunnels you want to give us," Ellen told the supervisor.

"Well, the second biggest tunnel is Family Life," he said.

"We'll take that one." Ben spoke up for the seniors.

"Okay," said the supervisor, "the freshmen group can take the Great Americans, Children Count . . ."

"How about the Spiritual Heritage tunnel?" Kate called out. She was concerned about the peacocks she saw last month.

Everyone looked at her, surprised she had a specific tunnel in mind.

"Sure," the supervisor replied. "Follow me to the maintenance garage. We'll get your supplies."

At the garage, each group received two buckets, two mops, a plastic jug of liquid soap, two step stools, some towels, and as many sponges as they needed.

The Park Supervisor laid out the project.

"Here's how to do it. There are restrooms next to each tunnel. Outside each restroom wall there's a water faucet with a hose on it. Take the buckets to the faucets and fill them with hot water. Add about a fourth of the soap into each bucket. The buckets have wheels on 'em. Roll the buckets back to the tunnel and *gently* wash the walls and the ceilings with a lot of soapy water."

"Will we hurt the paintings?" Derrick asked.

"No. Dont worry about it. After the artists painted the tunnels last summer, we applied a clear acrylic epoxy finish over the walls. It protects the paintings. But still, *gently* wipe them clean and dry them with your towels. Got it?"

All the SOULs nodded. Except one.

"What's clear, acrylic epoxy?" asked Alvin.

The supervisor was quiet. He wondered if he was being put on.

"It'll keep you from smearing the paintings," he finally said. "O.K.?"

Each group headed off to their assigned tunnels.

The four freshmen put all their supplies in the two buckets, which the boys steered with the mops.

Kate draped her arm around Alvin's shoulder as he pushed one of the buckets.

"Has there ever been a question that you didn't ask out loud as soon as it came into your really smart brain?"

Alvin didn't say anything. He just smiled and nodded.

There was one he had been wanting to ask her for over a month.

CHAPTER 7

HATE

MOVE OUT MEXICANS!   SCREW SLANT EYES
ARABS SUCK!   No AFRICA in AMERICA

"WHAAAAAAAT?" was all Alvin could say as he entered the Spiritual Heritage tunnel.

The four freshmen couldn't speak. The sight of the hate slogans took their breath away. Kate and Alvin had never seen anything like this. But the other two freshmen had.

"People are ignorant," said Serge. "I'm not surprised."

"No wonder they wanted to clean this up right away," said Kim Su.

"Scary," said Alvin.

"Typical," said Serge.

"Can't have visitors seeing this now can we? Oh my, imagine, racists in this wonderful city. Hurry, let's wipe all this away real quick before anyone gets the wrong idea." Kim Su's sarcasm was coming from deep within her. "Asian grocery stores and businesses get tagged like this every day. No one hurries to clean them up."

"They forgot a slogan," Kate responded. "'*Poor people are poor cause they don't hustle.*' But maybe they painted it in one of the other tunnels next to '*These people* are lazy.'"

"What's your PROBLEM?!" yelled Kim Su, her voice cracking. "Do you know what it's like to have your house tagged? You know how humiliating it is for everyone to walk by your house and see stuff like this written on your front door? Kids on the way to school in the morning, staring at *your* messed up house."

Kate heard the pain in Kim Su's voice. It reminded her of how her mom's voice had sounded when she talked about her dad. Kim Su couldnt stop.

"You know what it's like to leave everything you know and everyone you love to come to a strange place because your family has a dream that things will be better here? Then you get here and people hate you. Don't trust you. Embarrass you."

Kim Su took a few deep breaths.

Kate grabbed the mop and bucket, put her head down, and steered it to the faucet outside the restroom. Serge grabbed the other bucket and followed her.

When they were outside, Serge said, "When people hate you even when they dont know you, you get hurt. Then, after awhile, you get angry."

Kate kept walking.

Kim Su and Alvin waited in the tunnel, reading the slogans in silence.

If your parents weren't born here, you don't belong here.

WHITE POWER RULES!   **Forget Foreigners**

The slogans covered so many of the Spiritual Heritage images that it was difficult to really see the artwork.

"There's 13 slogans in here." Alvin told Kate and Serge when they returned with water in the buckets. He and Kim Su poured the liquid soap into the buckets. Everyone grabbed either a sponge or a mop and started cleaning.

Kate could see that Kim Su was still hurt and angry.

"I forgot," she told Kim Su, "something my dad used to tell me: 'Sticks and stones will break your bones but words *really* hurt.'"

It was Kate's way of reaching out. Kim Su understood and nodded.

Then Kim Su reminded everyone of the cleaning instructions they got from the Park Supervisor. "He said *gently* to remove the spray paint."

Kate went straight to the peacocks. Their message of inner beauty coming to the outside was blocked by "Move out Mexicans!" Kate began the careful work of restoration.

All the SOULs settled into their work; they did not talk much. A natural quiet seemed to descend on them. When they were finishing up around lunchtime and the images had re-emerged on the walls, the Spiritual Heritage tunnel was as silent as a monastery.

Until the vandals showed up.

CHAPTER 8

HEY!

"HEY, WHAT'S GOING ON HERE?!!!!" A voice yelled from behind the SOULs. It came from the city side of the tunnel. It was more than loud. It was angry and threatening.

Kate, Kim Su, Serge, and Alvin turned. Four figures blocked the tunnel entrance. The background light silhouetted the intruders as they marched shoulder to shoulder, like soldiers, toward the freshmen. Three guys and a girl, older than the freshmen, maybe eighteen or nineteen.

When they were within a few feet of the SOULs, the guy in the middle said it again in the same menacing tone, "What's going on here?!!!"

Alvin began explaining like he was answering a question in class.

"Well, we're from Kennedy High. We belong to a club, Save Our Urban Life, S.O.U.L. We help out here at the Park. And when we came today some idiots had tagged these tunnels with spray-painted hate slogans and . . ."

Serge grabbed Alvin's arm and stopped him. "I don't think they're interested, Alvin."

"That's right, camel jockey. We're not!" The guy next to the menacing voice sneered.

"We liked it the way it was," the third guy added.

"How do you know how it was?" Kate asked. Her tone of voice made the question an accusation. "Did you do this?"

"Not us," said the girl. "It was Frankenstein, Mickey, and the Pirate."

Superwoman handed her photo to Kate. The three other SOULs huddled around her. As they studied the masked characters posing in front of their work, the vandals smirked at one another.

Kim Su looked at the guy in the middle. "You and the Pirate have the same jacket. Forget to take it off?"

The smirks disappeared.

"Go back to the rice paddies and take all your slant-eyed friends with you," the Pirate said.

"You guys suck," Kim Su snapped. "Have you always been this stupid, or just since your mother threw you out?" She spit out the insult without a second's hesitation.

One guy kicked over Alvin's bucket, the water went everywhere.

The four vandals, their bodies tensed and ready, moved toward the SOULs.

Serge reached into his pocket, pulled out his cell phone, jumped in front of them, and snapped a picture.

The vandals stopped, as if being photographed had paralyzed them.

"Give me that," said the Pirate. He pulled a folding knife from his jeans' pocket and opened it.

Serge grabbed a mop and held it in front of him. Kim Su grabbed the other mop. They were ready to defend themselves.

Suddenly, a loud voice echoed through the entire tunnel, demanding attention. "HEY!"

The vandals stopped and turned. The SOULs looked up. Both groups were momentarily stunned.

A middle-aged African American man, an Asian woman, and a small boy dressed as Spider Man had entered the tunnel from the city side. The man left the side of the woman and the boy and moved quickly. Suddenly he was between Serge and his would-be attacker.

He smiled, looked each person directly in the eye, and asked with great interest, "What's happening, boys and girls?" He seemed lighthearted, at most clowning.

While Serge and his attacker stared at each other in silence, Alvin blurted out.

"These guys wrote hate slogans all over the wall and came back here to stop us from cleaning it up. They wore masks. Serge just took a picture of them." He paused and pointed to the one in the middle. "This one was a pirate and he has a knife."

The man's gaze followed Alvin's finger, but the knife had disappeared.

"Ah, it's a fight!" the man exclaimed, like he had finally found out what was happening.

"A fight we're gonna win," said the Pirate.

"I've seen a lot of fights," said the man, "even fought in a war." He paused, and then said in a puzzling voice, "It's always hard to tell who wins."

Then he continued quickly before anyone could say or do anything. "I'm sorry," he apologized. "I haven't introduced you to my wife Carole and my grandson, Anthony. Oh, and I'm Tap, a nickname I picked up in 'Nam. We're here for the children's Halloween party. Carole, Anthony, these are . . ."

He turned toward the freshmen and shrugged his shoulders, "I don't know your names. First names only, please."

The SOULs counted off, each hesitantly saying their name, but wondering if this was really the time for introductions.

He turned toward the spray painters, "And you folks are?"

One was caught up in the moment and mumbled, "Tom."

The others stared at Tom.

"What is this? A freaking United Nations meeting!! A black guy with a Chinese wife who knows what little Spider Man here is," snarled the Pirate.

"I'm Vietnamese," Carole corrected him.

"Who cares what you are! Just go back to where you came from!"

"Cincinnati?" asked Carole, in a playful voice.

Kim Su laughed but she was stared into silence by the Pirate. His eyes went from person to person, letting them know they were being threatened. But when his eyes came to Tap, Tap was smiling.

"Let's go," the Pirate commanded.

Superwoman walked over to Kate and grabbed the photo from her hand.

"This isn't over!" threatened the Pirate as they disappeared out the city end of the tunnel.

"You know, he's right." Tap said. "It's never over. You will have to face this stuff all your life. Best to figure out now how you want to deal with it."

CHAPTER 9

FOOD FOR
THOUGHT

"All this fighting business makes me hungry. Anyone for lunch?" asked Tap rubbing his hands together in anticipation.

"But Mr., er, Tap," said Serge, "we didn't fight."

"We didn't? Felt like a fight to me. And I'll tell you why. But I can't think when I'm hungry. I already know what little Anthony wants."

"Hot dog," said the boy, grinning through two missing teeth.

"What are you laughing at?" Tap asked Carole.

"Because of my new 'friend,' today I'm getting a salad—an *Oriental* salad," she laughed, deliberately pretending to stick her nose in the air.

"Come with us," she said to the freshmen. "I'll tap on Tap for four more lunches."

"Um, thanks, but we're supposed to eat with the other kids from our school at noon," said Alvin.

"Free lunch from the city councilwoman today," Kate added.

"Thank you, though," Kim Su said.

"I see you guys are all from Kennedy?" Tap asked Serge, who was wearing his gray hooded school sweatshirt.

"Yes. We are part of the Save Our Urban Life program there."

"Did you know that the whole SOUL movement was first started at Kennedy?" asked Tap.

"No," said Serge.

"Oh yeah, and there are SOULs in a lot of schools around the country now."

"1,285 schools," Alvin supplied the numbers, then added, "or something like that."

"Carole, okay if I visit with these SOULs for a minute and meet you and Anthony at the concession stand?" Tap reached for his wallet.

"No prob," she replied, taking the money from her husband.

"After you order your *Oriental* salad," Tap teased, "I'll take a hamburger. An ALL-American one! That's what I'm talking about!" He laughed.

Carole playfully waved him off. As she and Anthony headed to the concession stand, she called out, "Nice meeting you all."

"You too," the SOULs hollered back.

"So you were in Vietnam?" asked Alvin.

Tap nodded. "Since you won't have lunch with me can I offer you guys some food for thought?"

"Go for it," said Kim Su.

"You sure?"

"Yeah, yeah."

"Okay then, chew on this: When do you know darkness has turned to light? When do you know night has become morning?"

"What kind of question is that?" asked Alvin.

"A riddle," Tap admitted.

"When you can see things," said Kate.

"Yeah," said Tap, "but does darkness turn to light when you can see an elephant, or when you can see a koala bear?" His arm swung in a large circle as if to take in the entire Lincoln Park Zoo.

"Doesn't matter. As long as you can see it," Alvin said.

"And what if you think you see an elephant and it turns out to be a rhinoceros?" Tap replied. "Still daylight? Or is it night?"

"You have to be able to see everything clearly," said Kim Su.

"You're making a big request of light, Kim Su. To see everything clearly."

"What's the riddle, Tap? You said it was a riddle." Serge wanted to know.

"Drum roll, please," he said tapping one hand on the side of a bucket in a staccato beat. He waved for someone to join him.

Alvin reluctantly went along, tapping on his bucket.

"Here's the juice," Tap said. He and Alvin stopped drumming. "You know darkness has become light when you can look into the face of every person and see your brother and sister. Only then do you know night has become morning."

The SOULs were stunned. No one said anything for a minute.

"What about those who tried to ruin the tunnels? Those racists?" Serge finally asked.

"Misguided. Asleep. But under the masks, the Halloween masks and the ones they wear every day, they're the same stuff as us. They have names. The problem is they won't tell us and we can't find them out."

"They should go to jail," insisted Kim Su.

"Most likely they will," Tap agreed. "But they didn't win today."

"They tagged the tunnels and if you hadn't come by, they would have hurt us. I call that winning." Kate shook a little as she said it.

"They win if they turn you into themselves. When you are consumed by hate as much as they are, then they win. The real fight is to resist their hatred with good."

Then Tap turned to Serge. "Why did you take their picture?"

"I don't know, it just seemed the right thing to do," Serge replied. "It stopped them for a moment, didn't it?"

"Yeah, but then he pulled the knife," Kate reminded him.

"You did the right thing. Darkness fears the light. It doesn't want to be known. You don't fight darkness with darkness, you fight darkness with light."

"What are we talking about?" asked Alvin. "I'm lost."

"Hamburger time," laughed Tap, "then off to the haunted house. It's gonna scare Carole and I to death. But little Anthony the Spider Man is scare proof."

"Thanks for everything," said Serge. Then all the other SOULs chimed in.

"Thank you for cleaning up the Spiritual Heritage tunnel" Tap returned the gratitude as he turned and headed into the light. "I know I would have missed seeing the peacocks and all the other teachers."

Kate's mouth dropped.

CHAPTER 10

GADFLY

"Lunch is on the city today. Come on and get something to eat! My way of saying thank you."

Carl Howard had stopped by the Spiritual Heritage tunnel to remind them of the invitation.

"You all go ahead," Alvin told the group. "I'll be there in a minute."

Alvin was so shocked by the hate slogans and so absorbed in washing them off that he hadn't had a chance to look at the actual images in the tunnel. He took his time looking around, taking it all in alone.

But he wasn't alone long.

A man showed up at the far end of the tunnel. As he walked toward Alvin, Alvin could see he was middle-aged, wearing an opened overcoat with a buttoned sweater underneath. He had a drop cloth, a small step-ladder, and a tray of paint cans. He was carefully studying the walls. As he came closer to Alvin, Alvin blurted out, "Can anyone paint these tunnels?"

"Don't know," said the man.

"Did you have to get a permit?"

"Nope. I'm the one who painted all this in the first place. Did you see anything in here that grabs you?"

Alvin, who never misses a detail, missed the question.

"Sorry those idiots messed up your artwork."

"No big thing. They're not awake yet," said the artist.

"It's after twelve o'clock!"

"They're not awake," he said again.

"So are you here to fix something they screwed up?"

"Nope. Just want to touch up some stuff from the summer. But I see it's too late. They've got a protective coating on it."

"Where do all these pictures come from?" asked Alvin.

"From people who know the ways of spirit."

"Which image is the best?"

"The one that is a mirror."

"I don't get it. There are no mirrors."

"The one that you can see yourself in."

"What if you can't see yourself in any of them?"

"Keep looking." The artist saw that Alvin was stumped. "Sometimes help is needed, and help is always available."

"What kinda help?" asked Alvin.

"The kind of help given only to seekers."

"What's a seeker?" It was the eighth question Alvin asked.

"Follow me," said the artist as he moved down the tunnel.

"I have a hunch," he said, "that you ask a lot of questions, one after the other."

Alvin thought for a moment, and then what had long been pent up came out. "I can't stop. Everyone laughs at me.

My teachers ignore me. Even Kate asked me if I ever had a question in my head that I didn't blurt out loud."

Then Alvin said in a dejected voice, "They think I'm a pest."

"Actually, you have the makings of a particular type of pest—a gadfly." The artist laughed to himself at his little joke.

Alvin did not laugh.

"Look." The artist pointed to the wall where a small fly with extended wings hovered.

Alvin peered closely at the insect like he was studying himself in a mirror.

"Flies get a bad rap," the artist continued. "People always think they disturb contentment, ruin picnics, and so forth. Unfortunately, contentment is valued more than disturbance, especially when things need to be stirred up. Nothing stirs things up like the right question. So don't be too down on yourself."

"You mean asking questions is okay?"

"Of course, but I suspect you have to get better at it."

"Get better? I'm trying to stop it."

"Don't stop your strength. Bring discipline to it. It doesn't need to be denied. After all, you didn't choose it. You just happen to have an inquisitive mind. It's a gift that can help others."

Alvin was silent for a while, but he could sense the artist was perfectly comfortable with silence.

Finally, he asked "How do I discipline my questioning?"

"Ah," said the artist, "the right question. Notice when you paused and thought before you spoke, the question was more focused. And it seemed to mean a lot more to you. You said it in a completely different tone. Ask fewer questions and ask them more incisively."

"What's incisively?"

"It means more to the point or more to the heart of a situation."

Alvin was silent.

After a while, the artist said, "I love the sound of silence." Again he laughed a little to himself. "Any other questions?"

"Not right now. I'm thinking."

"Good answer. But, actually, I suspect you are pondering." He paused on purpose, seeing if Alvin would impulsively ask the next question. But Alvin was practicing his new discipline and held his tongue.

The artist smiled.

"I think pondering is the kind of thinking that moves from the head to the heart. Now, I have a question for you. Do you know who history's most famous gadfly is?"

"No."

"Socrates. He tried to get people to look more deeply at their life, and he did it by asking questions. He used questions to help people ponder."

"I've heard of him."

They left the image of the fly and then went on a tour of the tunnel. The artist pointed out five or six more drawings and explained their spiritual messages to Alvin.

"Thanks for cleaning up the tunnel," the artist finally said.

"Wasn't just me. Four of us did it."

"Tell them I said thanks."

Alvin had one more question. He tried hard to figure out if it was a worthwhile one. He was disciplining his strength. The artist let him struggle in silence.

"Which one is your mirror?" Alvin finally asked.

The artist smiled at Alvin's question. Without saying a word, he simply pointed to a white bear twirling a golden wreath on his paw.

CHAPTER 11

TO TELL OR NOT TO TELL

"Where's Serge?"

"Dunno."

Kate and Kim Su were standing in line for their free burgers and drinks when they noticed Serge wasn't with them. The girls glanced at the hot dog line and then at the pizza line. There was no sign of him.

They looked at each other and the same thought hit them at same time. Neither said it out loud, but both girls read it in each other's eyes. *Serge was smart enough to snap a picture and the first to grab a mop to protect his friends. But had the vandals come back for him now that he was alone?*

Kim Su and Kate headed back to the tunnel.

"Let's split up," Kate suggested. "You go toward the lagoon; I'll go toward the main gate. If we don't find him, then we'll meet right back here and tell Ms. A."

Kim Su nodded.

They walked off in opposite directions, but the more they thought about what might be happening to Serge, each girl began to run.

Within minutes they were back at the table, out of breath, and with no Serge.

"We have to tell Ms. A," Kate said in between deep breaths.

"I saw her by the supply garage," said Kim Su.

The two girls jogged toward the garage. As soon as they got past the restrooms, they saw Serge under a tree. He was kneeling on the grass, facing east, his forehead touching the ground.

The girls stopped immediately.

"Whaaaat?" Kate asked quietly.

"Noon prayer," whispered Kim Su.

Serge finished his prayers, stood up, and turned around. He was surprised to see Kate and Kim Su waiting for him. Together, they walked back to the lunch area. The long line was gone now. It only took a second for them to grab their food.

"I'm starving," Serge said. He ate steadily for a few minutes. Then he paused and said, "Can I ask you a question?"

"Sure," said Kim Su.

"How do you deal with it?"

"You mean moving here?"

"Nuh uh." Serge shook his head. "The prejudice against you. What you talked about in the tunnel."

Kim Su thought about it for a second. She wasn't sure whether she wanted to talk about it.

"I try not to let it get to me. Most of the time I believe that, down deep, most people are good. Like the goodness in people will show up. Only a few people are hateful or dumb or whatever."

Serge nodded. "I do the same. But honoring people is sometimes very hard."

"Yeah! On a bad day, I can do some serious dis-honoring." Kim Su laughed.

Kate laughed too, "I hear that!"

A voice inside her nudged her to admit her own struggle.

"I'm struggling right now to honor someone in my own family. I can't see his goodness. I'm angry all the time. Scary, right?"

Kim Su and Serge didn't know what to say.

Suddenly Ms. A appeared. "How'd you guys do with your tunnel?" she asked as she sat down next to them.

"Okay," they said, not sure how much they wanted to reveal. There was a pause.

Ms. A looked skeptical. A bland, one-word answer from three freshmen didn't feel right.

"You sure?"

Serge wondered how much he should tell her. He had a picture of the vandals on his cell phone, but he didn't want to get involved reporting a crime to the police. The Pirate said it wasn't over, but Serge wanted it to be over.

"Yes," Serge said.

Ms. A decided to let it go. "Well," she asked, "is the tunnel clean?"

The three freshmen nodded.

"And you've almost finished eating, right?"

More head nodding.

"You three are awfully quiet."

No one spoke. Each one was trying hard to wear their best "look innocent" mask on this Halloween afternoon.

"Where's Alvin?" asked Ms. A.

"In the tunnel," said Kate. "Now that we cleaned up all the graffiti, he wanted to study the paintings before we left."

"Can you go get him, Kate? I don't want him to miss lunch."

"Sure."

Ms. A then headed off to check on the juniors and seniors.

"You think we should have told her?" asked Kate.

Kim Su shook her head.

"This stuff happens all the time. It's best to forget it. We don't want those four coming back," Serge said.

"Besides," added Kim Su, "if we tell now, we'll have to explain why we didn't say anything right away."

"I guess so," said Kate, still not completely convinced. "I'm going to get Alvin."

CHAPTER 12

SWIMMING IN AND
SWIMMING OUT

"We meet again."

"I can't believe this!" Kate exclaimed as she walked past the concession stand on her way to get Alvin.

Standing directly in front of her were two little girls dressed as M&Ms, one red and one yellow. An older woman stood behind them like a guardian angel. It was the peacock party from last month!

"We went to the GAMES!" yelled the red M&M who recognized Kate immediately.

Kate bent down and looked at both of them closely. "I really like your costumes." Then in a voice pretending to be filled with maliciousness and hunger, "You look good enough to eat."

The M&Ms jumped back. The grandmother and Kate laughed. They walked together to a nearby bench. The girls played with some of their game prizes.

"I thought of dressing them as peacocks," the grandmother said.

"Funny you should say that. I was just in the tunnel cleaning graffiti off the peacocks. Actually, I've thought a lot about them.

A lot has happened since I first saw them. I know they're about . . ." Kate was looking for the words.

"Going to the inner beauty and bringing it to the outside," the grandmother helped. "Some people call it 'manifestation.' Others call it swimming in and swimming out. Actually, it's a form of praying."

"I thought praying was talking to God," Kate said hesitantly. Just like before with the peacocks, she wasn't sure she wanted to get into this.

"That's okay for M&M's" she replied as she patted the heads of her two M&M granddaughters. "But we when we get older, we need more."

"Why?"

"The journey gets more difficult. More issues to deal with, more things you have to do. We need to find a deeper strength. Prayer is deeper when we go inside and bring outside what we find there. Swimming in and swimming out."

Suddenly Kate remembered her mother telling her that she should pray to find a way to let go of her anger toward her father. Was this the way?

"Gotta go. The girls and I have a few more animals to visit. Good to see you again," the grandmother said with a smile.

"Bye." The M&M's waved.

All three began to walk away.

"Wait a minute," Kate called out.

The grandmother turned around. "Yes?"

"This wasn't a coincidence, was it? Meeting you and everything?"

"Some people think there are no coincidences," she said and smiled.

The two M&M's grabbed their grandmother's hands and pulled her down the path to the next game.

Kate just stood there for a couple of moments.

Swimming.

THE LION AND
THE LOTUS

CHAPTER 13

"Kate, you alright?"

Alvin had left the tunnel a few minutes earlier and was heading to join the others when he saw Kate. She was standing like a statue near the concession stand.

"I have to talk to Robbie," she said. "He's right. There's definitely something going on here."

"I just met the guy who painted the tunnel," said Alvin.

"Whaaaat?"

"Yup. Explained a bunch of the stuff to me, too."

Just then, Kim Su and Serge showed up.

"I just got a private tour of the tunnel by the guy who painted the whole thing!" Alvin repeated with some pride.

"For real?" asked Kim Su.

"He came back to touch up a few things. But he didnt know about the clear, acrylic epoxy finish." Alvin grinned at getting the words right. "Said all the pictures were teachers and told me about some of them."

Kate remembered that Tap had called the peacocks and the other images teachers.

"Why teachers?" asked Serge.

"They tell us something about our spirit, how it works, and how we should take care of it. We can learn from them."

The three other freshmen just looked at him, not sure what to think.

"I'm serious." Alvin could see the blank looks on their faces.

"I'll show you."

They went back to the tunnel. It looked like it had never been vandalized.

"We did good," Kate said.

"What's this mean?" asked Kim Su, pointing to a lotus flower surrounded by water.

"I asked him the same thing!" Alvin said. "The white flower is our soul and water is our body. I think I got that right."

Kim Su stared at it.

Serge had drifted further down the tunnel. He pointed to a reclining lion with a massive head and flowing mane. The lion had no front paws.

"This one needs help. He must have lost his paws when we washed off the spray paint. Did the artist see this?"

Alvin walked over to Serge.

"The guy said thats how its supposed to be. He told me the power of the lion can be out of control. But without paws, the lion tells us to use another type of power."

"What type of power?"

"I dont know," said Alan.

Serge said nothing but kept looking at the painting.

"And the artist said that these paintings are like mirrors," Alvin continued.

"Mirrors?" asked Kate.

"Yup. You will see yourself in one of 'em. Said we only understand the ones that show us to ourselves."

"Peacocks," Kate said simply, pointing to the two birds.

"Even the artist has one of these as his mirror." Alvin was loving his role as teacher.

"I'm going to tell Ms. A about the fight," Serge said out of nowhere.

"I thought you said no way," Kate said.

Serge looked at Kim Su. "It's this lion. The vandals want to fight with hate slogans and a knife. There's another way."

Kim Su nodded. "That Tap guy said the same thing: 'Respond to darkness with light.'"

Everyone was quiet.

Kim Su looked at Serge, "Let's tell Ms. A."

As they all headed out of the tunnel, Kate repeated something she had muttered to herself a few minutes ago.

"I've got to talk to Robbie."

CHAPTER 14

KNOWING
YOURSELF

"She's beautiful," Robbie whispered to Uncle Shaun.

"Inside and out," Uncle Shaun whispered back.

Robbie and Uncle Shaun were standing side by side at the front of the church with the groom and the other groomsmen. Robbie had been nervously fidgeting with his tux, but he forgot his discomfort as the organ music swelled. The guests in the pews stood, craning their necks and tilting their heads to see his aunt, Elaine, on the arm of his grandfather.

When they arrived at the front, the music stopped.

Robbie's grandfather lifted the veil from his daughter's face, kissed her, took her hand and gave it to Tom, the waiting groom. The ceremony had begun.

Robbie had never been this close to a wedding. The beauty and solemnity overwhelmed him. *No wonder they do this in a church*, he thought to himself.

Then he listened to the vows exchanged between Elaine and Tom.

"I promise to honor you and respect you all the days of my life," said Tom.

"I promise to hold you and stand by you all the days of my life," Elaine replied.

"In sickness and in health."

"For richer or poorer."

"In good times and in bad."

Robbie took his eyes off the bride and groom and looked at the guests. They were leaning forward in total concentration. Some were smiling, some were dabbing their eyes with a handkerchief or tissue. Everyone was hanging on each word of the bride and groom. When he heard, "You may now kiss the bride," Robbie turned back just in time to see it. The guests applauded.

"Very cool," Robbie whispered to Uncle Shaun.

After the wedding ceremony, everyone went to the reception. Robbie sat at the head table with the rest of the wedding party. It was a long table with everyone sitting on one side looking out at the assembled guests.

"When are you getting married, Uncle Shaun?" Robbie asked with a smile.

"It takes two, Robbie."

"Got any prospects?"

"Not at the moment," Uncle Shaun replied.

"How will you know when it's the right one?"

"Geez, Robbie, you are a bottomless box of questions. Give it a rest."

Robbie felt like he was Alvin, asking too many questions.

"Sorry," Uncle Shaun said after awhile. "Sometimes when the topic turns to, 'When are you getting married?' I feel pressure. People seem to have a timetable for me, but I know myself. I'll know my future wife when I meet her."

Robbie liked the confidence in Uncle Shaun's voice. It made him feel strong just to know him, yet the words "I know myself" triggered another voice. It was equally as strong as Uncle Shaun's.

Msfits appeared in his mind. She had told him something like that in the library a few days ago, "Truth isn't knowing what happened. Truth is knowing yourself."

CHAPTER 15

NO PLACE TO
HIDE

"I need to find the restroom, Uncle Shaun. I'll catch up with you later."

After Robbie had washed his hands, tossed the paper towel in the trashcan, and was heading out, he saw a pair of brown dress shoes sticking out beneath one of the stall doors. He was fairly sure he knew whose shoes they were.

There was no one in the other two stalls. So he went with his guess. "Dad? Is that you?"

The man in the stall blew his nose, twice. "Yeah, Robbie. It's me." His dad's voice sounded like he had a cold.

Robbie and his dad had come to the reception in the same car, but once things got started, he hadn't seen him.

When Mr. Matthews came out of the stall, Robbie saw that his dad had been crying.

"Dad? You okay?"

Mr. M nodded as he wiped his eyes. "Still got some grieving to do. Which is fine. Got to be honest with myself. Can't push away things just because they make me feel sad. It's just that this wedding reminds me of when your mom and I got married. She would've loved it today."

Two years had passed since Robbie's mom died and it had never crossed his mind that coming to a wedding would be so painful for his dad.

"What was you and Mom's wedding day like?" Robbie had never thought about it much, but now he really wanted to know.

"Amazing." Mr. M said with a sigh. Then he smiled

"Mom was gorgeous. When I saw her come down the aisle towards me, it took my breath away. I'm serious. I opened my mouth and the breath just came out of me. The groom's not supposed to see the bride before the ceremony, so I hadn't seen her in the dress yet. She was so beautiful. She was so happy and I was a nervous wreck. But your mom was calm and confident. She smiled at everyone, both my side and her side of the aisle. But halfway down the aisle, she looked straight at me. It was like nobody else was in the church. This beautiful woman that I loved so much was walking straight to me. I can still see that look in her eyes."

Mr. M took a deep breath, as if it might help him pull himself together. He blew his nose one more time and continued.

"The wedding today made me realize how much your mom and I went through together, and how much we hung onto each other. I'm sad that she's gone. But I would rather have had those sixteen years with your mom and have to say goodbye to her, than to never have had any time with her at all. And then to see you standing up there in a tuxedo, looking all handsome and grown up, made me so thankful that your mom and I had you. Geez, she loved you so much, Robbie. She would've loved to have been here today, to see you up there. But then again, I'm sure she did see it."

With that Mr. M tossed his paper towels into the trash can and started back toward the reception. But he noticed Robbie wasn't ready to leave quite yet. He was blowing his nose.

CHAPTER 16

GETTING A
SENSE OF IT

"Ready to go?" Kate asked.

"All set." Eric replied.

It was Halloween night. After spending most of the day at Lincoln Park, Kate was going bowling with her three friends.

The local lanes called it a Trick or Treat Bowling Party. The Treat was you could bowl all the games you wanted in 90 minutes for $3. Up to five bowlers a lane. The Trick was costumes were *required*.

When Kate came home from Lincoln Park, she had tried to call Robbie. She wanted to fill him in on what happened and what she was thinking about. But his cell went straight to voice-mail. She'd left a message for him to call her.

The more she thought about what happened at the Park—all the talk about who people really were—the more it seemed right to ask her brother Eric along. Kate's friends were cool with Eric being not only the fifth bowler, but since costumes were required, the fifth clown.

Kate could see how excited Eric was. This was way better than taking him trick or treating door-to-door like she did last year.

Those days were over. He was getting too big for that.

"Cool." Eric said as he and Kate finished studying themselves in the mirror.

"We're ready, Mom," Kate called out as she shifted the red rubber nose on her face.

Mrs. D put her arms around her two clowns as they headed toward the car.

"I'm going out tonight too," she said with a smile.

Kate stopped walking. "With who?"

The tone in her voice told her mom a lot. "Some friends from work," said Mrs. D, trying not to be specific. She knew what Kate was thinking.

"Is it a date?"

"Kate, relax."

They were silent for the entire ride over to the bowling alley. Kate worried her mom was moving on with her life and that her dad would be gone for good. She didn't even know how deep her feelings were until now. She couldn't look at her mom. She couldn't even speak. Even her clown face couldn't hide her sadness.

"Bye Mom!" yelled Eric, as he and Kate got out of the car in front of the bowling alley.

"Kate," Mrs. D called out, "Thanks for taking your brother along. Have fun."

"You too," Kate replied. It was hard for her to say it. But she did.

The bowling alley was packed and full of the loud sounds of bowling balls crashing into pins, music playing over the P.A. system, and kids laughing and rooting for each other. The party was on.

Eric, Kate, and her three friends got their bowling shoes and waited for their lane to open. Kate wondered how her brother would react to all the noise, action, and costumes.

"You okay?" she asked him.

Eric did not respond. He couldn't take his eyes off all the costumes—Jack Sparrow from the Pirates of the Caribbean; The Thing from the Fantastic Four; a Mummy; a Witch; Dorothy from the Wizard of Oz; Sponge Bob; Disney Princesses Jasmine, Ariel, Aurora, and Belle; even a Nun.

But once they started bowling, Eric focused on keeping the ball on the lane and not in the gutter. He thought clowns standing still were funny, but clowns bowling were hysterical.

On the lane next to the clowns were five juniors from Fenwick. By the second frame everybody knew everybody.

"Is that your brother?" one of them, named Brad, asked Kate.

"Yeah. That's Eric. What are you guys supposed to be?" Kate asked, trying to figure out their costumes.

"The Five Senses! Can't you tell?"

Kate didn't get it.

"See my big ears? I'm the sense of sound. Hearing!" Brad pointed to one of his friends. "See the big nose on Ryan there? He's Smell. Get it?"

Kate noticed one guy with big plastic lips with a red tongue sticking out. "He's Taste," she said. "The guy with the gigantic fake glasses is Sight, and your friend Tom over there, with the huge yellow gloves on his hands, is Touch, right?"

Brad nodded with a smile. "You got it. So, our costumes make *sense*. Get it? The costumes of the five senses make *sense*!"

"I get it," laughed Kate. "Funny."

"Your brother's having fun!" Brad said, bringing the conversation back to Eric.

"Yeah. He's too big to take 'Trick or Treating.' So I brought him bowling with us instead."

"How old is he?"

"He turned thirteen two weeks ago."

"That's not too old! I wish I could still go! I would load up a whole pillowcase full of candy," Brad laughed.

Kate grinned. "Yeah. But he's big for his age."

Brad nodded. "How many brothers and sisters do you have?" he asked.

"It's just me and Eric, and my mom," Kate said.

Brad got quiet for a moment. She wondered what had made him stop talking. Then she figured out was it was.

"My mom and dad broke up," Kate explained. It was her turn to bowl so she got up to retrieve her bowling ball.

As she waited for the lane to reset, Kate noticed that she didn't say *my dad left us* like she always did. Maybe she was cutting back on the blame, giving her dad some slack.

But she also said broke up, like it was a done deal, finished, over.

"Who's winning?" Eric asked loudly.

"Your sister!" his teammates yelled back after Kate got a strike. Kate sat back down next to Brad.

"There's a difference between good friends and friends who are good," she told him. Nodding over to her friends she added, "These are friends who are good."

The Sense of Sound didn't make any.

"How about yours? Are they good friends or friends who are good?" she asked.

"Little of both." He shrugged. "My mom and dad got divorced too," he blurted out.

Kate hadn't expected the sudden change in conversation. But she made the switch and was right there with it.

"At first you either want to scream at them both, or put all the blame on just one of them, or you just want to totally shut down so you don't have to feel any more anger or pain," he said.

"Then what happens?" she asked him.

"If they are people who are *good*," Brad said, "like your friends, you go back to loving them again."

She turned back to watch her good friends bowl. The Five Senses were now done and moving on.

"Hang in," the Sense of Sound said as he left.

"You too," Kate replied with a smile.

Later, when the Five Senses had gone, Kate retrieved a number on her cell from the Recent Calls Received.

There was someone she wanted to call when she got home.

CHAPTER 17

MAKING
THE CALL

"Thanks Sis." Eric took off his wig and nose.

"Fun, huh?"

"Big time."

Kate watched her brother head to his room. She knew he'd be asleep in a few minutes. She went downstairs, put the wigs and noses back in the Halloween box, and got a diet drink from the fridge. She plopped on the couch, grabbed the remote, and flipped through the channels. Nothing was on except Halloween horror movies. After almost an hour, she grabbed her cell and dialed the number she had been looking for back at the bowling alley.

It took several rings before the person on the other end picked up. With each ring she thought about ending the call.

"Hi Kate!" said the surprised voice on the other end.

"Hey, Dad. I just wanted to say Happy Halloween."

"Ha! You too. Get any candy?" he teased.

"I thought of you tonight," she said. "Thought about some of the funny times Trick or Treating. Remember the time when Mr. Schmieder pretended to be a fake mummy on his front porch?"

"Ha! He jumped up and scared you all to death!" said Mr. D.

Kate giggled. "We all screamed and ran over each other trying to get off the porch. But Eric just stood there! He was so scared he couldn't move!"

"I don't think he ever recovered," laughed Mr. D. "Do you remember the time the both of you dressed up as Ninjas?"

"Eric kept Kung Fu-ing everyone who opened the door."

"Yeah. Those innocent people thought they were being attacked for their candy stash! Like, Trick or Treat this! HIIGHY-AAAAH!!!!" yelled Mr. D.

"And you never told him to stop!" laughed Kate.

"Heck no. It was too much fun watching all those unsuspecting—'Oh aren't they cute, two little Ninjas'—grown-ups get mugged by a karate-chopping first grader. Are you kidding? I wasn't about to tell him to stop."

"How about the time the dog came running up the street toward us?" Kate kept the reminiscence going.

"Oh, I can't believe you brought that up! You two dropped your pillowcases full of candy and ran back toward the house. 'Forget the candy, run for your lives.'"

"Then the dog stopped and ate the candy," she gasped from laughing so hard.

"Tell me about it! You started to cry, so I was stuck trying to rescue the candy from that fire-breathing dog. Almost mauled to death trying to save my kids' Halloween loot!"

"We had fun tonight, too." Kate said.

"What houses did you go to?"

"None. We went bowling with my friends instead."

"Bowling?"

"Yeah. If you came in costume, you could almost bowl for free. So, me and my three good friends, and Eric went dressed as clowns. Eric had a lot of fun. It took him awhile to get used to seeing monsters and cartoon characters bowling."

"He probably thought he had stepped inside a movie or something."

"He did. It was funny. I was nervous at first. Not sure if it would be too confusing for him, ya know?"

"Yeah," said Mr. D.

"But he really did have a great time. Besides, he's getting too old to go Trick or Treating."

Kate's dad stopped laughing. For a second, she heard nothing on the other end.

"Dad?"

"Has he gotten taller?" asked Mr. D.

"A little. And his voice is starting to change."

"Really?!"

"And right after he started seventh grade, he stopped calling me 'Sissy.' It's 'Sis' now," Kate said.

There was a pause on the other end of the line.

"How you doing, Kate?" her dad asked.

"Good. School's good. Got good friends. It feels good being in high school now."

Kate and her dad talked for a few more minutes about her hardest subjects, her latest grades, and favorite teachers.

"I also joined a club called S.O. U. L. It stands for Save Our Urban Life. We work at the zoo once a month. It's been strange, but I've learned a lot."

"About what?" her dad asked.

Kate couldn't exactly name what she'd learned. And she was definitely not going to go into peacocks and coins. But somehow the reason she took Eric bowling and the reason she was talking to her dad on the phone right now was linked to that strange tunnel.

"About life," she finally said.

"Well," her dad admitted, "It's always good to learn about life."

Then Kate brought it up. The true reason she called. Brought it straight up. "I really missed you tonight, Dad, what with all the Halloween stuff going on."

"I miss you guys too. When you told me that all of you went bowling dressed as clowns, I thought sometimes I'm a clown for leaving. Maybe the sad clown. The one with the tear painted on his cheek."

There was silence.

"I'm gonna call Eric this weekend. For sure."

"Really? That would be good. Eric would love to hear from you."

"I promise," he said.

Then, just before they hung up, Kate heard her dad say something she hadn't heard in a long time. Something she really missed. When she heard it, it felt good, and right, and real.

"Love you too, Dad," she said.

CHAPTER 18

HIGHER
WISDOM

"I thought you'd be here."

Robbie turned around from the computer on the swivel chair. He immediately smiled, "Hey Kate."

It was Meatloaf Monday so Robbie had decided to spend the lunch period in the library working on the SOUL of The K website.

"Why didn't you call me back?"

"Was with my cousins and aunts and uncles all weekend. Wall to wall—all weekend with the wedding and all."

"How was it?" she asked. "Never heard of a wedding on Halloween."

"The wedding was greeeaat." A wicked smile appeared on his face. "The bride didn't lose her jewelry."

"Funny," Kate said.

"How was Lincoln Park?"

"Nobody jumped in the lake," Kate paid back.

"Ouch!" Robbie clutched his chest.

"Something bigger happened."

Kate told Robbie about the graffiti all over the Spiritual Heritage tunnel.

"*No way.*"

Then she told him about meeting the vandals and the fight that almost happened.

"No way!!"

Then she told him about the guy who stopped the fight from happening.

"Whaaaat?????"

"He was funny and smart at the same time," she explained.

Then she told him about Alvin meeting the artist.

"F'real?"

And Kim Su and Serge telling Ms. A and the cops the whole story.

"Really!!!"

Alvin suddenly appeared next to Kate. He had two books in his hand. "That's exactly how it happened, Robbie. It was very strange and I'm sure we're going to talk about it at the meeting after school today."

"I gotta put this on the website." Robbie spun around in the chair.

"Speaking of the website, you need to fix it," said Alvin.

"Fix what?" asked Robbie.

"You got some stuff wrong."

"Like what?"

"Like Richard Nixon," said Alvin. "Nixon was the president when the SOUL of The K was started. Not Johnson."

"Whatever."

"Serious. Details matter." Alvin insisted.

"Alright. Alright. I'll fix it," Robbie said as he swiveled back to the computer.

"And explain that the other stuff you mentioned happened a few years before the start of SOUL in '71." Alvin added.

"Who turned on the History Channel?" asked Kate "Robbie, I'm not finished. There's more!"

Robbie and Alvin turned back toward her.

"It's started again. That's why I called you right after I got back from Lincoln Park. Or maybe it never stopped."

"Being watched?" asked Robbie.

Kate nodded. "Way past being watched. We're being taught."

Kate paused to let it sink in. All weekend she had been mulling over the events of the last couple of months. Now she wanted to test her thinking out on Robbie.

"Put it all together," she continued. "It's like that puzzle at the front of the library. Piece after piece is laying around waiting for us to assemble it. We've known something is going on, and what is going on is we are being taught. The homeless looking guy tells you about the giraffe, my conversation with the grandmother about the peacocks, then the woman on the bus, and the emails, the backpack, the phone call, all the coincidences that are not coincidences. Someone is trying to tell us something."

Kate turned to Alvin. "I'm glad you're here, Alvin. You're a part of this. Look at Saturday. You were there when the guy 'Tap' stopped the fight and asked us if we wanted 'food for thought.' Then, the tunnel artist gives you a personal tour and explains a lot of the stuff to you. Whatever he told you about the water lily and the lion made Serge and Kim Su change their minds about not telling Ms. A and the police about the vandals. The artist called the paintings 'teachers.' That tunnel is the classroom."

Alvin pondered before asking, "What are we being taught?"

"Higher wisdom," Robbie answered immediately.

"What?" asked Kate. "Did you say wisdom."

"Msfits told me the angel on the coin was there to help me understand the higher wisdom of why I got the coin."

"Angel?" said Alvin.

"She said 'Truth' on the coin is not about knowing what happened. It's about knowing yourself. That's the higher wisdom. Kate, you're not learning about peacocks, I'm not learning about giraffes, and Alvin's not learning about . . ." Robbie paused and looked at Alvin.

"Socrates and gadflies." Alvin held up the two books he'd been carrying—*A History of Flies* and *Socrates: The Man of Questions*.

Kate and Robbie laughed. Then Alvin laughed.

When they quieted down, Alvin said "I think we have to find the artist."

"Or Msfits," said Robbie.

CHAPTER 19

AN
OLD SAYING

"We had a change of plans at the zoo on Halloween, didn't we? You all did a great job adjusting to the situation on the spot." Jamie Allister opened the SOUL after-school meeting on Monday. "And," she continued, "I think you all know we had a serious situation with the return of the vandals."

Everyone erupted.

Ms. A raised both hands to get the SOULs to quiet down. "And the freshmen did very well."

"Nice job," Ben congratulated them all.

"Good move, Serge."

Serge looked down a little embarrassed by the attention.

"So we have to do some reflection on it," Ms. A said. "But first, does anyone know what some people, like Catholics and Episcopalians, call today, the second day after Halloween?"

"All Souls Day," Ben blurted out.

"A perfect day for us to have a meeting!" Ms. A laughed at her own pun. "What a coincidence! SOULs meeting on All Souls Day."

"But the Original SOULs took the 'coin' out of coincidence," quipped Dana.

"So that means this meeting's over, Ms. A," said Derrick. "See ya."

Everyone laughed as the seniors pretended to get up to leave.

"Funny," Ms. A said with a big smile. She liked the easy joking. The SOULs were having fun but, more importantly, they were waking up.

"But seriously, since today is All Souls Day, I invited another SOUL in the school to join us. This person has been a SOUL longer than anyone else here at The K."

Ms. A moved to the classroom door and opened it. "I think you all know our guest," she said with a smile.

Msfits entered the classroom.

Immediately the seniors stood up like the President of the United States had just walked in. When the younger SOULs saw them stand, they scrambled out of their chairs.

"It's an honor to have you with us today, Ms. Fitzsimmons," said Ms. A. "Thank you for joining us."

"It's an honor to be with young SOULs," said Msfits. "I'm sorry to make such a grand entrance, but Jamie thought it would be fun." She paused, "It was."

The SOULs laughed with her.

"You all know Ms. Fitzsimmons as the librarian," Ms. A nodded in her direction. "But you may not know that after years of study related to her work in the library, she is an expert in the history of religions and sacred symbols."

Robbie nudged Kate, "She's our angel," he whispered.

"So I've asked her to tell us SOULs something about All Souls Day, something she thinks would be appropriate for Save Our Urban Life."

Msfits leaned against Ms. A's desk. "First, we should start with Halloween. For us Halloween is just fun. But originally Halloween was a time to recognize and ward off evil. I understand you had a run in with evil."

The SOULs became immediately quiet at the word evil.

When no one responded, Msfits asked, "Well?"

"Some vandals spray-painted all the tunnels with hate slogans," Dana said.

"Which tunnel did you clean, Miss Cali?"

"The seniors cleaned Family Life, the juniors did Workers of the World, and the freshmen worked on Spiritual Heritage. The vandals came back and the freshman almost got in a fight with them."

Msfits nodded and slowly her gaze moved from SOUL to SOUL, making eye contact.

"Now after Halloween, comes another day that is more important, but it's a day that evil tries to mask, one that evil tries to make people forget. Does anyone know what the day after Halloween is?" Msfits looked around.

Kim Su raised her hand. "Yesterday was All Saints Day."

Msfits nodded. "Here's how I see it, and it's no coincidence," explained Ms Fits, smiling after the last word. "For Halloween, some people tried to damage our families, our work, and our spirits with hate. But after that evil day, you spent the morning cleaning the walls, restoring them to the place of honor they deserve with your 'saintliness.'" Msfits said, making imaginary quotation marks around her last word. "Evil always tries to cover up goodness but love restores it. That's the truth you embraced from last weekend."

Msfits' two very old and very small hands came together, pulled apart, and came together again. She was gently applauding their actions on behalf of truth.

Soon all the SOULs were gently applauding.

"That brings us to All Souls Day. Yesterday was the day some people remember saints and today is the day they pray for everyone, not just saints, but all the souls who have died. They believe no soul is beyond reach and that all souls are related."

Msfits leaned forward from her perch on Ms. A's desk and repeated herself. "All Souls are related."

"Even the racist vandals who tried to hurt us in the tunnel?" Serge blurted out. It was the same question he had asked Tap in the tunnel two days before.

"The real fight is to resist hatred with good." Msfits smiled.

"I've heard that before," said Serge. "The guy who broke up the fight in the tunnel said the same thing."

"It's an old saying," Msfits smiled again.

CHAPTER 20

THE MYSTERIOUS UNIVERSE

"Msfits?"

As soon as he said it, Alvin had a stricken look on his face. A ripple of laughter went through the room.

Alvin cleared his throat before starting again.

"I'm sorry. *Ms. Fitzsimmons*, I meant to say. When Serge mentioned the tunnel, it made me think of all those pictures. Since we're SOULs, is there one that represents us?"

The SOULs groaned.

"That's an excellent question, Mr. Kline. I'm glad you asked it."

The groaning abruptly stopped.

"A bird is one of the most common images. It symbolizes the soul flying free when the body dies."

"There are birds all over the Spiritual Heritage tunnel," Alvin said.

"Even a fly."

Robbie and Kate looked at one another and smiled.

"Can a flower in water be a picture of the soul?" asked Kim Su.

"Yes," said Msfits, "It's a very popular image."

"The artist showed me that picture in the tunnel," Alvin said.

"You met the artist?" Several students asked at once.

"Yup. Kate, Kim Su, and Serge know. He showed up after the fight, um, not *fight*, but after the vandals left. I told him I was sorry that those punks, I mean vandals, messed up his work. He said they were still sleeping. I was like 'But it's lunchtime.' But he said 'They're not awake.'"

"Sounds like something Ms. A would say," Dana interjected."

"Sounds like something a SOUL would say," said Ben.

Ms. A saw an interest in the SOULs she hadn't seen before. This was a moment to be seized.

"I have an idea," Ms. A said. "A week from this Friday we have a half day off because of testing. Who wants to go to back to Lincoln Park to see this tunnel?"

Almost every SOUL immediately raised his or her hand. Ms. A went to her file drawer and pulled out a small stack of permission slips.

"Okay, we'll leave right after school and get back here by three-thirty. Make sure you have these permission slips signed and brought back to me a week from today."

Then Ms. A turned to Ms. Fitzsimmons, "Ms. Fitzsimmons has applauded our good deeds. Let us thank her for being with us today."

The SOULs, began to applaud, but Msfits cut them short.

"Might I have a last word?" she asked, and continued without waiting for a response. "Who can recite the Save Our Urban Life Mission Statement?"

While everyone else looked down, Alvin flipped open his notebook. In a loud voice, he said, *"We seek to serve urban life, not only the human, but plants, animals, the earth, and anything else living in or beyond the mysterious universe."*

Msfits slid off the desk.

"Well, when you go to the tunnel, you will be in the mysterious universe," she said.

Then she saw a raised hand.

"Yes?"

"Ms. Fitzsimmons?" Robbie asked. "Do you want to come with us?"

CHAPTER 21

THE CLOWN WITH A
TEAR

"Do I have everyone's permission slip?"

"Everyone who's anyone." Ben repeated his favorite line.

"Okay, let's head to the bus stop."

It was Friday afternoon and Ms. A was taking most of the SOULs to Lincoln Park.

"According to my schedule, the Number 12 bus passes by at 1:12 P.M.," Alvin announced. He looked at his watch. "That means we've got thirteen minutes."

"Quite organized," said Msfits. She was bundled in a hat and scarf.

"Thank you," said Alvin. "I get a lot of grief over being organized, and asking too many questions."

"But not from me," Kate teased.

"Yeah, right," Alvin replied.

Just as she did at the park, Kate put her arm around Alvin. "You know it's all in good fun. I wouldn't tease you if I didn't really respect you."

"Yeah right," he repeated.

"Seriously. You pay attention and stuff. The rest of us sort of just drift."

"Thanks," Alvin said quietly. He folded up his bus schedule and stuck it inside his coat pocket

1:12 P.M. came and went, but no bus.

"You sure you read that thing right?" asked Ben.

"You sure you have this year's schedule?" teased Derrick.

"You sure it's a Chicago bus schedule?" laughed Scott.

"Funny," Alvin said.

The Number 12 bus showed up three minutes late.

"Our boy here says that you are three minutes late," Derrick announced to the bus driver.

"Your boy's right. We had several special passengers to load up a few stops back." The bus driver nodded to three passengers in wheel chairs. "Takes a few more minutes."

With that, Derrick bumped fists with Alvin. "You had it right the whole time."

Alvin sat down next to the window. Kate plopped down next to him. Robbie and Msfits were behind them.

"See. I told you we all respect you," said Kate.

Alvin nodded as he looked out the window. Kate could sense that he was someplace else.

"What's up?" she asked him.

Alvin pretended not to hear her.

"What's up?" Kate asked him again.

"You used to avoid me on these trips."

Kate was surprised by his answer. But she knew he deserved the truth.

"Yeah, I did. It was pretty stupid. I was caught up with the whole image thing. Gotta look great. Gotta hang with the right people. All that. I even avoided my brother!"

"Everyone avoids their younger brothers and sisters," said Alvin.

"I avoided mine because he has Down syndrome. I was embarrassed to be seen with him. Too worried about my image. But I'm changing."

Alvin was surprised Kate was telling him all this. But it encouraged him to risk the question he had been waiting to ask. *The time is now*, he thought to himself.

"Can I get your cell numer?" The question rushed out like it had to be said fast or it wouldn't be said at all.

Kate was surprised, gave it some thought, and then she nodded. Alvin pulled his cell from his jacket pocket. Kate slowly recited each number.

"What's yours?" she asked him.

Alivin watched her punch it in, making sure she got it right.

As soon as Kate was done, her cell rang, as if on cue.

"Hello?"

"Hi Kate. It's me, Dad. The sad clown with the tear."

"Hi Dad. What's up?" she said as quietly as she could.

"I figured you were in class right now, so I was just calling to leave a message. Everything alright?"

"Everything's fine. Half day today, so I'm on a field trip right now. In a bus heading to Lincoln Park."

Kate could sense something wasn't quite right. Her dad's voice didn't sound right. Kate noticed a pause on the other end of the phone. She wondered why her dad had called to leave a message on her cell. She turned toward the aisle for a little more privacy.

"How are you doing?" she said automatically.

"Okay. But strange. After we talked on Halloween, I felt really sad. No, really bad. Kate, I just want to tell you that I'm sorry. Sorry that I caused you and Eric so much grief by leaving."

His words caught her off guard. For some reason, for a bunch of reasons, Kate started to cry. She couldn't help herself. And she couldn't answer. She just nodded a couple of times, as if her dad could see her through the phone. Finally, she whispered, "I know."

"I'm gonna let you go now Kate. I was just calling to leave you that message," Mr. D said, sensing his daughter's emotion. "And I'll call Eric tonight or tomorrow. Gonna' find out how he's doing and maybe tell him the same thing." He added, "Take care, Kate."

"You too." Kate turned off her cell and sat back, still half facing the aisle. Her tears made her feel free, but she was hoping no one noticed.

Then someone seated behind her gently placed a tissue on her shoulder.

CHAPTER 22

AN OVERTURNED PITCHER AND A BEAR

"Okay, this is our stop," Ms. A announced.

Everyone scooped up their backpacks and made for the door. Kate was still lost in thought.

"Kate! Your backpack," said Msfits, lifting it out of the seat as Kate headed toward the front of the bus.

Kate returned. "Thanks," she said. "For the tissue, too."

As the SOULs approached the Spiritual Heritage tunnel, they saw a woman standing at the entrance. She was waiting for them.

Ms. A ran ahead. "Mom! What are you doing here?"

"Well, you invited me to come didn't you?"

"Yeah, but you didn't tell me you were coming. I figured you couldn't make it."

"I wanted to see what the city was up to with these tunnels."

"Everybody," Ms. A waved the SOULs close. "This is my mother, Mrs. Katherine Allister. You may remember I told you all about her at the beginning of the year. I showed you her Kennedy High yearbook with the pictures of the original SOULs who started Save Our Urban Life."

A chorus of SOULs said "Hi."

"Cool yearbook," said Ben.

"Fun to go back in time," Katherine Allister replied. Then she walked over to Msfits and hugged her.

"When my daughter told me that you were going to make the trip, I just had to come and see you. You are the real reason I came. I think of you often."

"It's good to see you too, Katherine."

The two women spoke softly as they entered the tunnel holding each other by the arm.

"How are they doing?" Katherine whispered to Msfits.

"The younger ones are starting to awaken. See if you can pick them out," Msfits whispered back.

Inside the tunnel, the students dropped their backpacks and wandered around, looking every which way. Mostly, they were quiet. Occasionally, one would say, "Look at this!" and others would walk over to check it out.

"A tunnel of blessings. Each symbol tells a story," said Msfits.

Scott Belkat, a junior, ignored Msfits' comment. Eagerly looking at the freshmen, he said, "Tell us about the fight."

"The big army guy came in and the vandals ran away, right?" asked Derrick.

"Not exactly," said Kate. "He was sorta funny. It was like he was 'mc-ing' a show. He asked us to introduce ourselves."

"What about the graffiti guys? Whad' they do? Cuss him out?" Ben asked.

"One of them actually gave his name," said Kim Su, laughing, "but the leader, the Pirate, told him to shut up."

"Giving names makes things personal," explained Katherine Allister. "It's harder to fight when you have met the person."

Ms. A gave her mother a look that seemed to say "Give it a break. Don't go mystical-mom on me right now."

"Msfits, I have a question," Kate said. "Down here."

Msfits and the SOULs walked to the other end of the tunnel. Katherine Allister stood by the pile of backpacks, watching.

Msfits stopped and pointed to an image. She laughed. It was an overturned pitcher with water flowing out and down onto two pairs of feet. One pair had brilliant crimson painted toenails.

"You know who washes feet, don't you?" Msfits asked Kate. Kate nodded.

"Then you know the message: serve others."

Kate nodded, but her mind was on another image.

"Let me show you the one with my name on it. See if you can figure it out." She led Msfits to the peacocks.

"How the hidden is revealed. How the inside gets to the outside. How the feathers that are not seen are suddenly seen. The two peacocks belong together. This wisdom is called manifestation," said Msfits.

"Putting silver and gold on the outside can't match letting the beauty that is on the inside come to the outside. Can't match the real 'manifestation.' Is that right?" asked Kate.

"Correct." Ms Fits said, standing perfectly still and saying nothing more.

Finally, Kate said, "What's on the inside that is so beautiful?"

"The treasure buried in a field, the pearl of great price, the fountain that never dies, the gate of heaven," Msfits replied, saying each image slowly, like she was savoring the revelation it contained.

The words washed over Kate. They seemed to cleanse her eyes. She saw clearly what had only been a gut feeling. Without thinking, she said what she saw. "It's love, isn't it?"

"Yes."

Msfits turned away from Kate, leaving her with her thoughts. As she did, Alvin was right there.

"What about this? What's with this bear?"

Everyone looked at the great white bear lying on its side. One front paw was extended in the air twirling a golden wreath. The bear's eyes were closed and he wore a slight smile on his face.

"Well, what are bears known for?" asked Msfits.

"Strength," said Ms. A, unable to resist jumping into the discussion. But now she felt her mother returning a "Be quiet yourself!" look.

"A great white bear is a symbol of the power of goodness," Msfits said. "But there's more."

"The person who showed me the peacocks told me that there's always more." Kate had joined the group.

"It's true. There's always more," Katherine Allister said, sticking her tongue out at her daughter when no one else was looking.

"What else are bears known for?" continued Msfits.

"Hibernation," said Ben. "They can live for a long time on the food they have stored up."

"Perhaps that's why his eyes are closed," said Msfits "He could be focusing on inner resources, food that sustains him."

"But what about the golden wreath?" asked Kim Su.

"That's a symbol of fulfillment. The good bear is offering spiritual resources to people as the inner food they need to grow."

"The artist told me this bear was the mirror in which he saw himself," said Alvin.

"Oh?" asked Msfits. "Then he was telling you he is a spiritual teacher."

Kate turned to Robbie and Alvin.

"I told you! We're being taught!"

CHAPTER 23

MIX IT UP

"What's all this?" Robbie asked.

It was Monday morning, and the cafeteria tables and chairs were arranged in small groups.

"Today is National Mix It Up at Lunch Day." Alvin supplied the answer.

"What's that?"

"Something new. Started like three years ago. High schools make kids sit with different kids at lunch for one day out of the whole year. Step out of your circle kinda thing. Like 9,000 schools do it with about 4 million kids. Here, you have to sit at a table based on the last letter of your last name. Each table has two letters on it, like that table right there," Alvin continued. "See the D and T. The idea is to get to know people you never hang around with."

"I get it." Robbie nodded.

He headed for a table labeled "S" and "O." Kim Su and Kate were already there.

"Matthews reporting to Vans and DiGiacomo," he announced.

Kim Su saluted.

Then Serge Henbatis plopped down with them.

"Uhm, I can see that we're really mixing it up," Kate teased. "Only one not here is Alvin!"

Soon the table filled up with five other freshmen and sophomores. But Kate looked around to see where Alvin was.

Alvin found a table labeled "E" and "P." He was the first there. As soon as he sat down, he wondered if he made a mistake. What if no one else came? He would be there alone. Everyone would be looking and laughing. But the table quickly filled up.

Seniors from the Student Council were at each table. Their job was to have everyone introduce themselves and then answer three questions. If you didn't want to answer a question, you could say "pass." But you could use "pass" on only one of the three questions.

The first question was: "What's the most embarrassing moment you've had since school started?" As the kids shared their stories, table after table filled with laughter.

"Walking into the boys' bathroom by accident the first week of school."

"Going to third period Math when it was really second period English."

"Asking my parents to transfer me to another school after practically dying in Mr. McKinney's first PE class!"

"Having to ask my English teacher how to spell the word literature."

"Not knowing where Spain was on the map in geography class."

"Having Msfits tell me that I should know to use my 'indoor voice' in the library."

"Dropping the glass bottle in chemistry class."

With the second question "What's the hardest thing you've had to deal with this year?" the bursts of laughter subsided.

By the third question, "What's the most important thing you've learned outside the classroom?" there was little or no extra noise in the cafeteria, only the sounds of voices in normal conversational tones.

"High school brings change. Even changes you don't really want. To be honest," said a freshman named Andres, "I'm glad I came to The K. It's a good school. Strong academics. A lot of different programs and stuff. Teachers are sharp. People are nice. All that. But I really miss my old friends. We used to be close. Tight. Me and a girl from my eighth grade class are the only ones who came here. All my old friends go to their school's football games together and whatnot. But I don't want to go to some other school's games. So like now, I don't even see my old friends on the weekends much any more. For real."

"I was learning something the hard way: Don't fall behind in your grades, no matter what!" a sophomore named Barb said, shaking her head.

"Keep honorable perspectives, drop dishonorable ones," said Kim Su.

"Good music will get you through," said a sophomore named Eli.

"Seeing ahead," said Robbie. "Like how the decisions you make today can affect you later." He paused, trying to find the right way to say what was in his heart. "And who a body is is more important than how a body looks."

"Sometimes you have to move on, even if you don't want to," said a sophomore named Rachel. "I got cut from the basketball team two weeks ago. Was on the freshman team last year but didn't make the JV this year even though I went to all the summer camps and workouts. I've been playing all through grade school. Now it's over. I was crushed. Still am."

Serge passed.

"I was gonna ditto something Robbie said," shared Kate. "But after what Rachel just said, I have to say, 'Me too.' Learning how to move on while still honoring the people or person making you give up something you really cherish. This has been huge for me."

The bell rang, and everyone grabbed their stuff and headed to their next class. But Kate jumped up and went straight to Alvin. She caught him before he left. Robbie grabbed her stuff and followed her.

"How was it?"

"Been expanding my circle," Alvin said with a smile.

"Did you answer all three questions?"

Alvin nodded as he grabbed his stuff.

"Call my cell tonight. Tell me what you said. You still got my number, right?"

"Will do," he said, trying to sound casual. But he was stunned.

Kate swirled around, intending to go back to her table to grab her backpack. But Robbie was holding it up in front of her. She nearly smacked her face into it.

"Expanding *my* circle," she said softly to herself.

"I hear you," he said.

CHAPTER 24

CONTACT

"Finally!"

Robbie had finished his homework and was working on the SOUL of The K website. He wanted to complete the story of last week's Halloween project. The title was *Trick or Treat*, and it gave an account of the entire day, just as Kate and Alvin had described it to him. He ended it with: *So the SOULs here at The K are trying to get in touch with the artist who painted the Spiritual Heritage tunnel. If any of you SOULs out there can help us, we'd be grateful.*

After posting the summary, he received this e-mail from a.soulinPhilly: *Found this in the newspaper recently (Attached)*

He opened the attachment and found this newspaper article:

Most Hate Crimes Based on Race

WASHINGTON (AP) – Racial prejudice lay behind more than half of the hate crimes reported to the FBI. Information supplied by 12,711 local law enforcement agencies reveals that the number of race-based incidents rose about 5 percent last year.

65% of all racially based hate crimes were against African Americans. From Sept 11, 2001 until 2004 the percentage of hate crimes against Muslims has dropped from 12% to approximately 4%.

Robbie, King of the Kennedy website, responded.

Kweb: *Mind if I post this on our website?*

a.soulinPhilly: *Go for it.*

Then Robbie saw a message from OS.

He pushed his chair away from the computer and stood up. His eyes never left the screen. It had been well over a month since OS had sent a message, but Robbie had not forgotten the last time.

Before he had told anyone, OS knew Robbie had jumped in the pond after Kate's backpack, caught his shorts on an underwater branch, and been pulled free by someone. As Robbie read the message, he wondered if OS again knew stuff nobody else knew.

OS: *And if I helped you find this artist, what good would that do? Would it answer the questions that matter most?*

Robbie ignored that question and asked another.

Kweb: *How did you know about my getting tangled up under water at Lincoln Park back in September?*

OS: *Let me try this again: And if I helped you find this artist, what good would that do? Would it answer the questions that matter most? Time to say Goodbye again.*

Robbie's fingers flew over the keyboard:

Kweb: *Wait!!! The answer is NO. Knowing who the artist is will not give me or my friends answers to the deeper questions. But it may help us get in touch with more experienced SOULs. And that may be a way for us to get better answers to the deeper questions.*

OS: *Give me an example of a deeper question.*

Kweb: *Why did I get a coin?*

OS: *That's a good question. But only you can answer it. Answer that one and I'll consider answering one of your detective ones.*

Kweb: *I'm not totally sure why I received a coin, but I think it has something to do with coming to know a Truth about myself and doing something about it. I had gotten into some bad habits. Then I began to see where they were leading me. Like a giraffe, I saw long range.*

Robbie stopped typing. He replayed his bad habits in his mind. But he was not going to put them into this message.

Kweb: *So I <u>saw</u> what the problem was, <u>judged</u> it to be wrong, and took some small steps to solve it. I <u>acted</u>. That's what the coin is about. Plus, I think maybe I nurtured the spirit of a friend.*

Robbie waited a couple of minutes, but there was no response. Then, he headed toward the fridge and found a left over piece of roast beef. As he snacked in front of the TV, a message popped up on his computer screen.

CHAPTER 25

CHANGE

"I'm sick of this! Totally sick of it!"

Mrs. D turned off the TV. She was so angry she was talking out loud to herself. To Kate. To anyone who would listen.

"Another Special Report on school shootings! Last time it was hate crimes. Before that it was about Internet predators! Next time it will probably be about terrorist alerts. I'm sick of it! What is wrong with everybody? Where's the love these days?!"

Kate was at the kitchen table finishing her homework. Without looking up, she chimed in, "I agree."

But her mom wasn't finished.

"This is not the way it was meant to be. We're all related, for God's sake!! This evil stuff has got to stop." She loaded her dessert plate into the dishwasher.

Kate hadn't seen her mom this angry in a long time.

"We were talking about that at school . . . ," Kate said.

"I mean what's the deal? Can't people see that we should all try to get along? What ever happened to taking care of each other and 'Do unto others as you would have them do unto you'?

I'm telling you Kate, I hope you and your generation stick up for what's right."

"And that would be?" Kate asked.

"That would be things like charity, kindness, fairness, justice," Mrs. D was talking as she made her way out of the kitchen and up the steps to her bedroom, raising her voice the farther she got from the kitchen "respect, good will, hospitality, understanding." Her voice finally trailed off as she entered her bedroom.

"What's Mom mad about?" asked Eric as he came downstairs.

"Too much hate in the world," Kate said.

Kate was sticking books into her backpack.

"Coming to my soccer game on Saturday? Last game of the season."

Kate had missed most of Eric's matches.

"Definitely. I'm there."

"Sis," Eric's voice changed. "I don't want to ask Mom, she seems mad right now. But I spent all my money for the week. Could you lend me two dollars?"

"Yeah. Sure. I've been collecting a bunch of change in the front pocket of my backpack. Like two weeks of change. Go ahead and get it from . . ."

Just then, the house phone rang. Kate picked it up in the kitchen at the same time Mrs. D answered it upstairs.

"Um. It's me." She heard her dad say. There was silence on her mother's end.

"Mom, do you have it?" Kate asked.

"I got it, Kate." Her mom said calmly.

"Hi Kate," said her dad.

"Hi, Dad," Kate said. She was happy that he called like he said he would. She put the phone down.

"DID YOU SAY DAD!?" asked Eric.

"Mom's talking to him upstairs," Kate nodded.

Eric dropped the handful of change he had pulled out of Kate's backpack onto the kitchen table and ran upstairs.

"DAD?!!!" he yelled.

Kate began to tell Eric that he didn't have to go upstairs, he could just pick up the kitchen phone. But the noise made her turn. All her change was rolling off the table onto the kitchen floor. She bent down to pick it up, but suddenly stopped. Among the change spinning on the floor was a bronze coin.

Even before it came to rest she knew what it was.

TO BE CONTINUED.

TURN THE PAGE FOR A SNEAK PEEK OF BOOK 3

The Lincoln Park young adolescent mystery series includes:

Readiness

"You think they're on to us?"

"Wrong question."

The four figures in the Spiritual Heritage tunnel laughed.

It was a bright, cold Saturday morning in mid-November. The four had come together, spent time contemplating the images, and now were ready to look ahead.

"Wrong question or not, do you think they're on to us?"

"The giraffe knows more is going on than meets the eye."

"It's only a matter of time before the gadfly's questions start zeroing in."

"When I last saw the peacock, the look on her face said she was putting it together."

The four went back to the images, looking at them as if there was a revelation there they had yet to consider.

"A brick's coming out of the wall over here."

The brick was part of a yellow cross, and it was sticking out of the wall about three inches.

"Pull it out."

Behind the brick was an empty, rectangular space.

"Water must have washed away the dirt behind it."

One of them placed the brick back into the wall, but it didn't fit in all the way.

"Should stay."

"Not all the pieces ever fit perfectly anyway."

The four were silent.

"It's time for the right question. Are these kids ready to go to the next step?"

"Each is different, but each is ready."

All heads nodded.

"Then how should we go about it?"

"The brick that almost fits may have the answer."

They all laughed and said together, "Elizabeth."